Meet Piggy Handsome!

Just look at that hair!

This guinea pig has so much charm, and such flair.

And yet, he's not FAMOUS!

How it hurts! How it hounds him,

when portraits of famous old Handsomes surround him.

But here's a new plan, there's no way he can lose:

he'll save someone's life, so he gets on the news!

Will Handsome FINALLY revel in glory?

Let's see! Turn the page! And on with the story!

Piggy
Hero

Handsome's heading for glory!

Written by **Pip Jones**

Illustrated by **Adam Stower**

For two handsome little fellas,

Noah and Gus. xx

First published in 2018
by Faber & Faber Limited
Bloomsbury House, 74–77 Great Russell Street
London WC1B 3DA
Typeset by Faber & Faber Limited
Printed and bound in the UK by CPI Group UK (Ltd)
Croydon CRO 4YY
All rights reserved
Text © Pip Jones, 2018
Illustrations © Adam Stower, 2018

A CIP record for this book is available from the British Library
ISBN 978–0–571–32756–0

FSC
www.fsc.org
MIX
Paper from
responsible sources
FSC® C101712

1 3 5 7 9 10 8 6 4 2

1

Rooflessness!

or How to definitely not be a hero

At the top of a very tall building, in the centre of a blustery little town called Gibblesby-on-Sea, a pompous, puffed-up guinea pig named Piggy Handsome was about to push his best friend off a roof.

Again.

It's not *quite* as bad as it sounds. Nearly ... but not quite.

'What did I JUST say, Jeffry?' Handsome demanded, his perfectly coiffed quiff billowing in the breeze.

The little blue budgie rolled his eyes, tucked his wings in place, and sighed.

'You said: "no flapping".'

'Actually,' Handsome shrieked, 'I said: "ABSOLUTELY no flapping", Jeffry. And you flapped! You *must not flap*. It's very important. Let's go through the plan again.

'One: I push you off the roof.

'Two: With ABSOLUTELY *no flapping* of your wings, you plummet towards the ground.

'Three: I heroically dive off the roof after you, scoop you into my paws, activate my parachute, and lower you safely to the ground. Meanwhile, all those humans over there –'

Handsome gestured dramatically towards a large crowd that was gathered far below, in front of the building next door.

'– they'll turn around and gasp! And they'll

say, "Ooh, *look!* That amazingly brave and handsome guinea pig just saved a tiny, weedy little bird's life!" And they'll take photos of me on their phone-thingies and send them to the Internetist, and they'll ring up Gibblesby TV News. And then, FINALLY, everyone in the world will know who I am!'

Yes. You see, Jeff 'falling off a roof', and then Piggy Handsome 'saving his life', was all part of Handsome's latest plan to get famous. Every one of Handsome's ancestors (and there were eighteen generations before him) had been famous for something or other. Pottery, gymnastics, magic tricks, archery . . . well, the list went on and on.

Yet Piggy Handsome himself had never had his name in the papers, or on telly, or even on the internet. Not *once*. And so getting famous was the only thing Piggy Handsome really cared about. Well, that and his friend Jeff – though you'd have had a job getting Handsome to admit it.

Anyway, back to the plan.

Handsome had picked the perfect spot on Padlock Road – an already gathered crowd, waiting restlessly for something or other to happen next door, was just what he needed. Handsome was getting impatient, but Jeff was looking quiet and . . . thoughtful.

'The trouble is, Handsome,' Jeff said after a moment, 'I think your plan is flawed.'

'How *dare* you!' Piggy Handsome blustered, his ginger fur bristling. He wasn't really one for being told his ideas were anything less than fabulous.

'For a start,' Jeff continued, 'when you say "parachute", do you mean this thing?'

Jeff tweaked with his beak, picking at the elastic band that was awkwardly fastened around

Piggy Handsome's middle. It was attached to a paper carrier bag, which had a hole in it.

'It's a perfectly good homemade parachute, as well you know!' Handsome replied, batting Jeff's beak away. 'You even saw me testing it at home.'

'What I saw you do was jump off an upturned toilet roll and land on a soft rug without hurting yourself and—'

'Twice!' Handsome interrupted.

'*And,*' Jeff pushed on, 'an upturned toilet roll and a soft rug ain't quite the same thing as a five-storey building and a concrete pavement.'

'I can't see it's all that different,' Piggy Handsome argued, stretching his elastic band. 'And anyway, the point is, this would be a perfectly good plan if you just STOPPED FLAPPING! Let's try again. Ready?'

'Fine,' Jeff tutted.

Jeff took his place on the edge of the roof, looking out towards the docks and the glittering sea beyond.

Handsome took two steps back, then crept towards Jeff. He paused and ... pushed.

'HUFFT!'

'Tweeeeeeeeeeet!'

Jeff tumbled over the edge. He plummeted, as instructed, for precisely half a second, and then . . .

'Sorry, Handsome.' Jeff shook his head as

he landed neatly back on the ledge and tucked his wings away once more.

Piggy Handsome looked ready to erupt.

Madder than a poked eye.

'I told you to STOP FLAPPING!' he yelled.

'I can't!' Jeff protested. 'It's budgie instinct. Whenever there's air between my claws and a solid surface, my wings flap. They do it by themselves! They simply won't let me fall. You can't fight instinct, Handsome. It's a law of nature.'

'You and your *instinct* … and your silly … fluffy … WINGCOMPOOPS!' Handsome ranted as he marched back and forth along the ledge, his fists clenched in furious little balls.

'I think you're doing it deliberately! You don't even *want* me to get famous, do you? After all the things I've done for you! Don't forget I actually *did* save your life once. You're just not trying hard enough, Jeffry . . .'

That was when it happened.

Piggy Handsome tripped on a snail that was happily squelching its way along the ledge.

(Quite what a snail was doing on top of a five-storey building, I don't know – but snails do crazy things when they've had one too many dandelions.)

Anyway, tripping when you're on the roof of a high building is never a good idea. As you'd expect, Piggy Handsome went right over the edge, legs akimbo and everything.

'EEEEP!'

'Handsome!' Jeff gasped.

As he fell, Piggy Handsome tugged hard on his elastic-band-carrier-bag-parachute – but the bag bit refused to open, and instead just plastered itself to his ear.

Jeff swooped as his friend plummeted towards

the ground. He'd just managed to grab a piece
of elastic in his beak, when it snapped. Piggy
Handsome squealed as he disappeared into the
leafy branches of a horse chestnut tree and . . .

'HPPT!'

bounced

FLOMP!

all the way

'EEP!'

to the

DUFFT!

ground.

'Handsome? Oh, Handsome! Are you all right, pal?'

Piggy Handsome's eyes slowly opened.

'EEEEEPPPP!' he screamed, when he saw Jeff's eyeball two millimetres away from his own. Jeff hopped back a step.

Bewildered, Handsome looked around sleepily.

Blink.

Jeffry's beaky blue face.

Blink.

Bright lights.

Blink.

Cages.

Blink blink.

Cages.

Blink blink blink.

Rows and rows of cages!

They were filled with all manner of sad-looking creatures, wearing bandages and plasters.

'Good grief!' Handsome managed weakly. 'Where am I? Is this ... PRISON? Get me out! I can't be sent to prison! Help! Help! Heluuuurrrr ...'

As it happened, it was not a prison at all.

It was, in fact, an animal hospital – and

Jeff was about to explain as much to his friend, but Piggy Handsome's eyes had already closed once more.

Scoundrelous!
or A terrible rumour turns out to be true

Talking of prisons, there was an important reason why such a large crowd of humans had gathered on Padlock Road that morning.

The building they were standing in front of, as sad and blank as a broken old telly, really *was*

a prison. And while Piggy Handsome was being tended to in animal hospital (for a bump on the bum), the humans were still anxiously awaiting confirmation of a *terrible* rumour they'd been spreading among themselves.

CLANK.

A huge metal door whined open, hushing the murmurs of the crowd.

The prison governor stepped through, looking very serious — and possibly a little bit ashamed of himself. A bead of sweat trickled down his damp pink forehead.

'Right, well, er . . .' he said, clearing his throat. 'I've come out here to confirm that, yesterday, two prisoners escaped . . .'

The crowd gasped noisily, sucking in the odd passing fly.

'The runaways are twin brother and sister, Dan and Dolly Dixon, the hotdog van villains who were jailed for the notorious StickEmUpDownUpDownShakeEmAllAround Sticky Fingered Stick-Up at Jones's Jewellery Store.

'If you spot Dan and Dolly,' the governor continued, holding up a photo and turning it so everyone could see the villains' grimacing faces, 'you are advised not to approach them, but to call Gibblesby Police Station immediately.

'Thank you.'

The governor turned on his heel and scurried back through the metal door, which was slammed shut with another metallic

CLANK.

Greensleavers!
or Time to make a break for it

'Well it jolly well looks like a prison to me!' Piggy

Handsome bellowed, as Jeff fluttered over and

expertly opened his cage with a happy

PING!

'Good morning, Handsome!'

'There's nothing good about it! These cells are *abominable*. You can't just lock animals away like this – it's outrageous. And another thing . . . ouch!'

Handsome, who'd just woken up after a full day and night, hobbled out of his 'cell' rubbing his bottom, which had been neatly bandaged.

'No, no,' Jeff chuckled, 'like I tried to explain yesterday before you dozed off, Handsome, this isn't a prison, it's a hospital. A nice sort of human brought us here after he found you under that tree. I had to do a LOT of sneezes to make sure he brought me too. Anyway, the lovely nurse here looked at your graze and . . .'

'It IS a prison!' a croaky old voice came from across the room. 'Definitely a prison!'

'Banger? Is that you?'

Jeff flew over to a long, dark cage in the corner, and used his beak to unhook the hook.

An elderly sausage dog v e r y s l o w l y
made her way out on her stubby little legs.

'It IS you, Banger!' Handsome gasped when
he saw his neighbour from Elms Avenue. 'Oh!
My poor, ancient, wrinkly little friend! They've
imprisoned you too? We have to do something,
Jeffry. This is no place for a frail old thing like

Banger. It's dreadful here! There's a carrot in my cell and it isn't even *grated*! We have to break out of this den of doom, and get home at once.'

'But it's a *hospital*,' Jeff sighed, 'so Doctor Vethead will have to agree you're well enough to leave before . . .'

'Prison break!' Banger yelled. 'They can take our temperatures, but they'll never take our freedom!'

At 102 years old (in dog years, that is), Banger was looking far more excited than was probably sensible.

'Stop encouraging him, Banger,' Jeff tutted.

'You know very well this is a hospital. Why else would you be wearing that heart monitor?'

Jeff was right, of course. Banger did know exactly where she was – and she *hated* it. So if Piggy Handsome was willing to break them out of their 'prison', well, she was IN!

'I'll just get this, er, "tracking device" off, Handsome,' Banger wheezed. She used her long snout to remove the heart monitor, which was strapped around her chest. 'You two unlock the cells. We'll start a revolution! Once I've ... had a little ... sit down!'

'You can't just go letting them all out . . .' Jeff

began, but Piggy Handsome was already working

his way along the rows of cages, unhooking hooks

and heaving heavy bolts.

'Dear furry, and feathered, and – *yeurgh! scaly* –

little friends!' Handsome exclaimed (shuddering

just a little at the sight of a miniature python and its flickering tongue). 'Run! Fly! Or, er . . . slither! Be free!'

One by one the creatures emerged – confused, but happy for the chance to stretch their legs and wings and scales a bit.

'What's the plan then?' Banger croaked, her dark eyes shining beneath her tufty grey eyebrows.

'The plan,' Handsome whispered, 'is to—'

'RIOT!' Banger shouted.

'Fine, I give up,' Jeff sighed. 'But if we're "breaking out", I reckon sneaking through reception to the only exit might work better than a riot, Banger.'

'You're right, Jeffry,' Handsome agreed, peeping round an open door that led to the reception area. 'We just need to get past all those humans sitting on the chairs, and that human there behind the counter, and then smash through the glass doors using our fists . . .'

'Hmm,' Jeff said, peeping round the door too. 'One thing at a time, Handsome. Let's start with the sneaking bit. There must be at least twelve humans out there, and it's all open plan. There aren't any plants to hide behind or anything. Oh! I know what to do, I'll—'

'Ssshh!' Handsome interrupted. 'I'm thinking, Jeffry.'

'I just thought I could—'

'Ssshh!'

'You know how I can do that thing—'

'Ssshhh! I've nearly had an idea!' Handsome hissed. 'Yes, I've got it! You know how, when you're not squawking, you can do that strange mimicking thing?'

Jeff Budgie rolled his eyes.

'I don't squawk, I *tweet*,' he corrected. 'But yes, like I was going to say, I could—'

'You could make a noise to distract the humans!' Piggy Handsome squealed, clapping his paws together. 'I suggest you make the noise of a herd of elephants. Or a *meteor*. Something to scare them all away.'

'I think I've got a better plan,' Jeff replied. And before Handsome could argue, the tiny blue bird opened his beak and ...

... out came a far-away, thin and tinny sounding tune called 'Greensleeves'.*

In other words, the unmistakable sound of an ice cream van.

* If you've ever been told by an adult human that the slightly sorrowful 'Greensleeves' tune means an ice cream van has run out of ice cream (and some definitely do this, *fact*), I'm afraid to tell you that you were fooled. 'Greensleeves' means no such thing. That wicked old human just *didn't want you to have an ice cream*. What ... an absolute ... *PARSNIP!*

Ah, Jeff knew humans all right!

'Ooh!' They all gasped, digging pudgy hands into pockets and bags, for jingling-jangling coins.

'I could do with a cone . . .'

'A warm day like this . . . !'

'I wouldn't say no!'

'Strawberry or cola?'

'I'm having a flake!'

'Huphuphuphuphup!' Handsome chuckled. 'Quick, animal comrades! Get out of sight!'

As the humans stood to leave, picking up their

poorly pets, Handsome and Jeff ducked back around the corner and hid.

They waited.

And waited.

And waited, until the last walloping footsteps could no longer be heard.

'They've gone!' Handsome said, dashing out into the bright reception. 'Gosh, I really do have the most marvellous ideas, don't I, Jeffry? Now, we just have to smash our way to freedom!'

Jeff fluttered over to Piggy Handsome,

who was glaring intently at an enormous glass door in front of him.

'That glass must be five centimetres thick,' Handsome said gravely, 'but fear not, Feather Face, I can get us out of here with some Kung-fu I learned from my Great Uncle Chan Zen Handsome . . .'

'Or you could just . . .'

Handsome was already on the move.

'HYYYYYYYWWWAAAAAAAA!' he squealed, doing a flappy paws thing, as if there was an invisible wasp attacking him.

Two steps in to Handsome's 'Kung-fu' display, the glass door suddenly went . . .

SHHHHWWWWEEEEET

and opened wide. The fresh air rushed in.

'Good grief!' Handsome exclaimed in delight. 'I didn't even have to kick it! I just willed it to open. Do you know, I think I must have *actual super powers!*'

Well, of course, Piggy Handsome, who was now standing right underneath the motion sensor, hadn't seen the automatic door in action when all the humans had left.

'Yup. Super powers. *Definitely*,' Jeff said, sticking one leg in his feathers (which is the budgie equivalent of grinning, in case you didn't know). 'I've always suspected as much, Handsome. Let's go, shall we? You coming, Banger?'

Behind them, dear old Banger had only made it as far as the first door. Her nose was just poking through.

'I'll catch you young fellas up,' she shuffle-puffed. 'It might take me a while on these creaky old legs, but I'll see you back by the pond in your garden! We're freeeeeeeee!'

'Right you are!' Jeff shouted back to her. 'Come on then, Handsome. Let's see what other super powers you discover on the way home.'

Twinsensitivity!
or The rudest rapscallions in town

Piggy Handsome and Jeff strolled through the flower beds, unnoticed by humans who skipped and skated and cycled along the smooth grey path.

Apart from one outburst of rage, when

Handsome failed to make a tulip wilt just by staring at it, all was quiet. Everything on the East side of Pickering Park was birdsong-butterfly-peaceful.

The same could *not* be said for the West side of Pickering Park.

Close to the duck pond, in a sticky little place called The Boss Cafe, two *very* odd looking customers were giving the owner a right rude talking to.

'I wanted JAM doughnuts!' screeched a tall, scrawny woman with a grey beard. 'These ones are custard. They're 'orrible!'

'And this milkshake's got bits of fruit in it!'
yelled a short, plump man, who had glasses drawn
on his face in felt tip. 'Yeurgh!'

'It's a strawberry milkshake, like you asked
for,' retorted the old woman behind the counter.
'So of course it's got strawberries in it.'

'Well take 'em out, they're *disgusting*,' the man
said. 'And bring us some chips.'

She might have been elderly, but the white-
haired, bespectacled lady wasn't called Mildred Boss
for nothing – and she wasn't about to stand for this sort
of nonsense either. Her voice went all headmistressy.

'I will bring you some chips, young man, when you say "Please may I have some chips, Mrs Boss." *Nicely.*'

There was a pause.

The man shuffled on his feet and finally muttered: 'Can I have some chips, Mrs Boss ... NICELY please?'

'Ha! Big ninny!' the bearded woman quietly snorted.

'That's more like it,' Mildred said, as she smoothed down her greasy apron. 'But can't you read?'

'Huh?' said the man.

'Eh?' said the woman.

Mildred was pointing at a big sign on the wall that read: 'NO DOGS ALLOWED'.

Ah, yes! The dog.

In the man's chubby hand was a lead. And at the end of the lead was the most magnificent dog you could imagine.

She was gigantic – almost as tall and wide as the man himself. Her fur was pure white, and it was as thick and puffy as a *cumulonimbus* cloud. The dog's black eyes shone cleverly, but her expression,

well, it was ever so solemn.

'It ain't a dog!' the bearded woman blurted, snatching the lead suddenly. 'It's a . . . cow! One of them rare breeds.'

'Oh!' said Mildred, peering over her spectacles and squinting. 'Well, in that case, take a seat.'

Letting the creature lead the way, the man and woman found a table in the corner.

'Blast! Its spots have rubbed away again,' the woman whispered. 'And its horns have fallen off as well. Quick, pass me that lump of coal and two more bananas.'

The man rummaged in his pocket and passed the woman a lump of coal. The woman checked no one was watching, then used the coal to smear wide black spots all over the dog's coat.

'This thing's gonna make us rich!' the man sniggered as he tied two bananas to the dog's head,

angling them to look like cow horns. 'I told you this was a great plan. The silly mutt didn't even bark at us when we nicked it from the garden.'

'I know, ain't it brilliant!' the woman replied. 'All we have to do now is wait for its owners to bring us all that lovely dosh! What are you going to buy with your half?'

'Thirty-eight pinball machines and two tonnes of chocolate!'

'I'm gonna get a dog!'

'But we've already got a dog! Or is it a cow?' The man scratched his head.

'Not this dog, potato brain! I'll get a different dog. I want a tiny little scrawny one, which bites people's ankles and . . .'

FLOMP!

Their conversation was interrupted when Mildred plonked a gargantuan bowl of steaming chips on the table.

'The Boss special,' Mildred announced cheerily. 'That'll be nineteen pounds and fifty pence. Oh, plus your milkshake and doughnuts . . . I'll bring you your bill in just a jiffy!'

'Yes, do *please* bring us the bill!' the lanky,

bearded woman called in her best posh accent.

When he'd finished chuckling, and spitting bits of half-chewed chip all over the table, her companion joined in.

'The bill! Oh *marvellous*! We shall be most delighted to ... er ... pay it! HA! HAHA!'

They had no intention of paying it, of course.

These ruffians were as rude and grubby and lawless as they come.

You'll have guessed by now who they were.

None other than escaped convicts Dan and Dolly Dixon, wearing terrible (yet apparently surprisingly effective) disguises.

Behind the counter, Mildred busied herself with totting up what the Dixons owed.

At the table, Dan and Dolly chomped and guzzled, as noisy as pigs at tea time.

Underneath the table, the magnificent dog gave a sad sigh. She opened her enormous mouth. Out from it dropped a silver-grey rock, which landed with a

C-CLACK

on the floor.

'Right, let's get out of here,' Dolly said, 'before

that old bossy boots brings the bill!'

Dan stuffed another handful of chips in his mouth and stood up. He heaved at the huge dog's lead, while she picked up the rock once more. They were almost at the exit when Dolly stopped in her tracks.

''Ere, look at this!' she said.

Dan joined her to peer at a noticeboard on the wall. Among the handwritten adverts for nearly working vacuum cleaners and wheel-free bikes, there was a poster that read:

LOST!

Beneath was a photograph of Piggy Handsome, with Jeff peeping out from behind him.

And the scrawl said:

My beloved Piggy 'Poo Poo' Handsome and Jeff Budgie are missing from home.

If found, please return to 39 Elms Avenue, Gibblesby-on-Sea.

Thank you.

'I don't believe it!' Dolly exclaimed.

'What?' said Dan.

Mildred was suddenly behind them. 'Aw, yes. The lady was in here just half an hour ago putting up that poster. She's gone and lost her little pets, poor lovey. Anyway, here's your bill!'

Dolly snatched the piece of paper and sneered: 'Thanks *ever* so!'

When Mildred had returned to the counter, Dolly leaned in to Dan.

'Don't you recognise it?' she whispered, prodding the poster. 'That's the flea-ridden fluff ball from the hotdog van.'

Dan looked blank.

'Remember?' Dolly continued. 'He squeaked, and then let the handbrake off, and we rolled down the hill and crashed . . .'

'Er . . .'

'And then the police came and took all the cash and jewels off us . . .'

'Erm . . .'

Dolly was losing her patience.

'And then they THREW US IN JAIL!' she shrieked.

'Oh . . . *yeah*!' Dan nodded as it all came flooding – or rather, trickling – back.

'And it's all this stinking rodent's fault! *That hamster put us in jail!*'

Jailing the dastardly Dixons really *had* been down to Piggy Handsome in a way – although, the truth was, he'd never intended any of it.

'Ooh,' Dan grinned, 'and now we know where he lives! Let's *get* him!'

'But he's not there, is he?' Dolly tutted. 'He's *lost.*'

'Oh, that's right. Well, I ain't going round looking for him,' Dan groaned. He rubbed his tummy. 'I think I've eaten too many chips.'

'I'll bet there are posters up all over town

by now,' Dolly said. 'Let's just go to his house and wait 'til someone brings him home.'

'And THEN we'll get him!'

'Yeah!'

'Brilliant!'

Dolly screwed up the bill Mildred had given her and tossed it on the floor. Then she grabbed the enormous dog's lead and shouted: 'LEG IT!'

Dan and Dolly ran off through the park, cackling horridly and leaving poor Mildred Boss twenty-four pounds and fifty-nine pence down on her day's takings.

As if Dan and Dolly Dixon cared about Mildred Boss. Usually, there was only one thing on those fiends' minds, and that was money.

Today, though – oh, dear – there were *two* things on their minds.

Money ... and REVENGE!

5

Pupportunity!

or Someone really *does* need saving

'NGNNNNNNNNNEEEEEEE!
HYYAAAWWWAAAAYYYYYAAAW-
WAARRGHHHHHHHH ...'

Jeff was standing by the lavender bush, with
one leg in his feathers. For the last twenty-three

minutes, he'd been watching Piggy Handsome trying to open the front door of their house – with nothing but his brain.

It wasn't working.

'AAAARGHHH!!!! NGNNNNNNEEEEE! NGNNNNNNEEEEEEEEE!'

'It's no good, Jeffry.' Handsome puffed, exhausted from his effort. 'It seems my super powers don't work any more.'

Jeff could have told Piggy Handsome the truth about the automatic door at the animal hospital. And he could have told him that the front doors of houses don't have motion sensors, because otherwise burglars would just go round robbing people whenever they felt like it.

But the chance to see Handsome trying to open a heavy wooden door with his brain had just been too good to miss.

Now though, Jeff was starting to feel a bit bad.

'It's all gone wrong, Jeffry!' Handsome wailed. 'It was going to be brilliant! I was going to be your *hero*! My name should have been in all the papers this morning. I should have been on my way to Gibblesby TV News for an exclusive interview by now.

'But no. All is lost. I've even lost . . .' Handsome gave a sad little gasp, '*my super powers.*'

'Maybe you just need to re-fuel, Handsome,' Jeff suggested. 'Come on, let's go in through the window and get some grub.'

Piggy Handsome huffed and heaved himself up the flowering wisteria. Then he hopped through the top window, which was slightly ajar. Jeff fluttered in after him.

Inside the room they shared, with its bookshelves and pot plants and abandoned spider's web, someone was waiting for them.

No, no. Not the Dixons. It wasn't *quite* that bad.

'MRRrrrrroowwwl.'

'Tweet!' Jeff flew immediately to his ornate birdcage and slammed the door shut.

'Cranky Scrapper!' Piggy Handsome exclaimed.

He squared up (quite foolishly, you might think) to the manky black cat, with her glass-green eyes, and her raggedy, scraggly ears.

'What are you doing in here? This is a cat-free zone!'

If only. Handsome had tried to explain to his human that allowing Cranky into this room could put his and Jeff's lives in grave danger.

But, as always, all the human had heard was: 'EeepEeepEeepEeeeeeepEeeepEeep!'

She'd just kissed him on the nose.

So he'd bitten her.

Anyway, the truth was Cranky Scrapper was

far more interested in tormenting Piggy Handsome than she was in eating him. She drummed her jagged claws on the wooden floor.

'Your bottom looks bigger than ever,' Cranky taunted. 'Are you wearing a nappy?'

'How *dare* you!' Handsome retorted. 'It's a bandage! My bottom's just a bit swollen and—'

Cranky talked over him.

'Oh, so your plan to jump off a roof went just as I expected then! I didn't hear anything about you on the news this morning. Of course not. Poor little *Piggy*. No one is paying you any attention, as usual. You'll never be famous, because you're . . . *boring*.'

'Boring? *Boring?!*' Piggy Handsome's fur bristled 'til it was sticking out at all angles. 'I . . . I'm not . . . I'll have you know I can do the Cha-Cha!'

Handsome demonstrated that he could do the Cha-Cha by actually doing the Cha-Cha.

As you can imagine, a guinea pig doing the Cha-Cha is quite a sight to behold. Handsome's top half remained perfectly still, whereas his bottom half was suddenly all swirly hips, and double steps, and oomp-poompy pelvis lurches.

'Er, are you all right, Handsome?' asked Jeff. 'You look like you're about to do yourself a mischief.'

'Is the Cha-Cha boring, Cranky?' Handsome demanded. 'No! It most certainly is not. It is extremely, very, very UN-BORING!'

Cranky Scrapper yawned.

'I can hear something in the back garden,' she said flatly. 'I'm going to go and glare at it.'

Cranky turned to leave. Out of breath, Piggy Handsome finally stopped gyrating and collapsed in a little, fluffy heap.

'Good riddance!' he yelled after the cat as she slunk through the door. 'And don't come back, you big . . . PEANUT!'

'Well done, Handsome!' Jeff chirped, letting himself out of his cage. 'Phew, I'm glad to see the back of her. She's got a heart as black as burnt toast, that one. Fancy watching the darts?'

'No, thank you,' replied Handsome glumly. 'I think I'll just go to my maisonette and read the morning newspaper. Perhaps it'll give me an idea, for tomorrow.'

'Fair enough.' Jeff fluttered to the corner of the room and tweaked a button on the telly, which then fizzed into life. 'Adverts,' he tutted.

Inside his extravagantly decorated maisonette (a two-storey cage, really), Piggy Handsome grumpily flicked though the pages of the newspaper, muttering.

Jeff rolled his eyes, and tried to concentrate on

the darts match which had now started.

'Huphuphuphuphuphuphuphup!' Handsome giggled suddenly.

'Something funny, Handsome?' Jeff asked.

'Look at this, Jeffry!'

Handsome held up the newspaper to show his friend a page with the headline:

SPOTTED! Pet cow takes a
stroll in Pickering Park!

Then he read the story out loud:

Locals were amazed and enthralled yesterday to see a pet cow being walked around Pickering Park on a lead! Matilda Snappit, of Nosey Road, managed to take this extraordinary photograph.

'I was very surprised to see a cow in Pickering Park,' Matilda told a *Gibblesby Herald* reporter. 'Usually, you only see dogs on leads, don't you? Well, I said that to the owners, and the woman who was holding the lead shouted: "Well it definitely AIN'T a dog! IT'S COMPLETELY AND UTTERLY A COW! A RARE BREED OF COW, ALL RIGHT PEA BRAIN?"

'And so I asked what the cow's name was, and she said: "BOG OFF."

'So there we have it, BOG OFF really is a cow! Strange looking cow though. Smelled a bit funny, too. Like bananas.'

Have you also spotted BOG OFF while strolling around Gibblesby? Email your photos to us: bog-off@gibblesbyherald.com

'Huphuphuphuphup!' Handsome chuckled again. 'A cow on a lead! How extraordinary.'

'Hmm,' Jeff said, with one eye on the darts. 'Watch this, though. Biff Biggins could win – he just needs a bullseye and . . .'

Suddenly the darts match disappeared from the screen.

'Wha . . . ?' Jeff flapped his wings in horror as the TV cut to a news reporter. Handsome peeped round the door of his maisonette to watch.

'*Gibblesby TV News* interrupts your programme to bring you this newsflash,' the reporter said seriously. 'An extremely valuable dog – which is reportedly worth one and a half million pounds – has been stolen from a back garden in Gibblesby, and is now being held for ransom.'

'How terrible!' Piggy Handsome gasped.

The TV showed a photograph of the huge dog, while the reporter continued:

'Bunty Mastiff is an incredibly rare, pure white Tibetan mastiff, and is the largest of her kind in the world. A moment ago, Constable Shift of Gibblesby Police gave this statement.'

On screen, a skinny policeman with red hair and an upturned nose was standing in front of a crowd of reporters.

'Bunty Mastiff's owners received a ransom note yesterday morning,' Constable Shift said gravely. 'The criminals who stole the dog, whoever they are, are demanding six hundred thousand pounds for her safe return.'

Constable Shift held up the ransom note. It was made using letters cut out of a newspaper, and read:

GiVe us six hundred grand by Friday, or the dog gets it! Call our mobile phone to arrange. Number is 076 66666. TA.

The policeman added: 'We have advised Bunty's owners not to give in to the villains' demands. Gibblesby Police Force is committed to solving this crime. But if any member of the public has information that could help us ensure Bunty's safe return, we ask that they contact the police station immediately. Thank you.'

'Poor Bunty Massive,' Handsome said, shaking his head. 'Absolutely dreadful business.'

'Hang on a sec,' Jeff blurted. 'Show me the photo of that cow again.'

Handsome held up the newspaper and

Jeff fluttered over.

'That's not a *cow*, it's *Bunty Mastiff*!' Jeff exclaimed.

'Really?' said Handsome, examining the photo again himself. 'But the horns . . .'

'They're bananas!' Jeff jabbed the photo with his wing. 'And look at the humans! Don't you recognise them? She's wearing a fake beard, and he's got felt-tip glasses on. It's those two dodgy characters you accidentally got sent to prison, remember?'

'Ohhhhhhh,' Piggy Handsome said, squinting at the grainy picture.

Suddenly, Jeff was all aflutter.

'This is your chance, Handsome,' he exclaimed.

80

'Bunty Mastiff is already in the paper and on the telly. If you save *her* from her kidnappers, you'll be a proper hero, and then you'll definitely be—'

'FAMOUS!' Piggy Handsome squealed, running in circles. 'Quick! Quick! Quick, Jeffry! Let's ... hang on, how do we go about saving Bunty Massive exactly?'

'Well,' Jeff said thoughtfully, 'the first thing we need to do is find that small phone thingumajig our human's always looking at.'

Plantastic!
or What could possibly go wrong?

Now would you believe it? While Piggy Handsome and Jeff were ransacking their human's house, looking for her mobile phone so they could contact Bunty Mastiff's kidnappers, those very same kidnappers, and Bunty Mastiff herself, were actually climbing over the wall into the back garden.

'OOFFT! OW!' Dan Dixon fell flat on his rugged, round face, straight into a patch of thistles.

'EEERK! ME BUM!' Dolly Dixon squawked,

as she plunged into a rose bush.

Bunty landed as silent as a secret on the ground next to them, then sat down in the shade.

'Right, let's have a look through the window and see if the pinny gig's home,' Dan said.

'*Guinea pig*, not pinny gig,' Dolly hissed.

'Whatever,' said Dan, pulling thistle spikes out of his bushy eyebrows. 'Question is, what are we gonna do to him when we get our hands on him?'

'I know!' Dolly cackled. 'We'll stick him to a plate with sticky tape, and then we'll post him to the jungle, with a label tied to his toe what says

"TIGER FOOD"!'

'You're 'orrible!' Dan roared.

'And you're terrible!' Dolly roared back.

'And there ain't no villains like the Twin-Twin
Dixons!' Dan chanted.

'Yeah! Come on, bruv', let's DO IT!'

'Do what?'

'Get the flamin' rodent, you nitwit!'

'Oh, yeah! Brilliant!'

★

Dan and Dolly crept towards the back of the house.

Dan peered in through the back door window,

while Dolly tried the door handle.

'Drat, it's locked!' she said.

'I hate it when that happens,' Dan moaned. 'People are so selfish.'

'Well, how are we gonna get in?' Dolly asked.

'Go through the cat flap,' suggested Dan.

'You go through the flamin' cat flap!' Dolly shrieked.

'Me?' Dan said. 'I'm too big. You're the skinny one, you do it.'

'No, you do it!' Dolly argued.

'You!'

'You!'

'You!'

'You!'

'You!'

'You!'

'You!'

'You!'

'You!'

'You!'

'You!'

'You!'

'You!'

'You!'

'You!'

'You!'

'You!'

'*You!*'

'*YOU!*'

'FINE!' Dolly yelled. She knelt on the ground,

stuck her head through the plastic cat flap and . . .

'MRRRAAAOOOWWWWWLLLLLLL!!'

Cranky Scrapper, who'd been silently glaring at the Dixons through the cat flap ever since they'd tumbled over the wall, swiped with her paw (claws and all).

'Waaaahhhhhhhh!'

Dolly's head re-emerged. 'Cat swiped me brilliant beard!' she screeched.

BEEPBEEP!

Dan gasped and rummaged in his baggy trouser pocket. He brought out some chewed chewing gum, then a hanky with snot on it, then a slice of lemon meringue pie, then a broken yo-yo, then an old battery, then someone's else's toothbrush, then a very small bottle of ketchup,

then a caterpillar, then a crowbar, then a sausage, and finally, a phone. He wiped some crumbs and gunk off the screen, and used one stubby finger to prod a button.

'It's not the police again, is it?' Dolly groaned. 'Telling us to give ourselves up or else?'

Dan squinted at the screen.

'No,' he replied. 'It's a message from an unknown number. It says:

Dear Dreadful Villains,

Meet us in the depot at the docks at 5.30 pm, and bring Bunty Massive with you.

You'll recognise me because I'll be wearing something fabulous.

My friend will be wearing . . . feathers.

We'll bring . . . well, it'll be *quite* a lot of money. It might not be the full six hundred thousand pounds you've demanded, but we'll get as close to that amount as we possibly can.

And we'll give all of it to you, in exchange for Bunty's safe return.

See you at 5.30 pm then.

Toodlepip!

'YES!' Dolly pumped the air with her fist. 'I knew this plan would work! We're gonna be stinking rich!'

'Let's go!' cried Dan. 'We'll come back for the rodent tomorrow. Today, we've got a ransom to collect. Nearly *six hundred thousand pounds!* Woohoo!'

Impromptu-tu!
or Dressing for an unexpected occasion

The afternoon sun streamed in through the bay
window, illuminating a million specks of dust,
which danced prettily in the air.

'So how much money DO we have?' Piggy
Handsome called from inside his walk-in wardrobe.

Jeff finished counting the coins in the bowl on the windowsill.

'Nearly four quid,' he chirped. 'So not *very* close to six hundred thousand.'

'Better than nothing!'

'Cor, this could be exciting!' Jeff was hopping from claw to claw. 'I'm in the mood for a proper adventure. Saving a giant dog from two vile, wicked, *dangerous* villains ...'

Handsome emerged from his wardrobe, suddenly looking a bit pale.

'What's wrong, Handsome?' Jeff asked.

You might well think Piggy Handsome had just realised this whole thing was a *terrible* idea. A guinea pig and a tiny budgie? Taking on the dastardly Dixons? Any guinea pig in its right mind would stop for a moment and think: 'Actually, I'm a guinea pig. *What am I doing?* Perhaps I'll just stay at home and eat some cabbage.'

But no, it wasn't that.

'I have nothing to wear!' Handsome howled. 'And I absolutely CANNOT go *naked*! My purple and gold one-piece would be just *perfect* for a rescue mission – but I can't fit it on over this STUPID

THING!' He pointed at his bulky bum-bandage.

One by one, Piggy Handsome tossed all of his

seventy-nine outfits on to the floor . . .

'NO ...! NO ...! NO ...! NO ...! NO ...!

NO ...! NO ...! NO ...! NO ...! NO ...!

NO ...! NO ...! NO ...! NO ...! NO ...!

NO ...! NO ...! NO ...! NO ...! NO ...!

NO ...! NO ...! NO ...! NO ...! NO ...!

NO ...! NO ...! NO ...! NO ...! NO ...!

NO ...! NO ...! NO ...! NO ...! NO ...!

NO ...! NO ...! NO ...! NO ...! NO ...!

NO ...! NO ...! NO ...! NO ...! NO ...!

NO ...! NO ...! NO ...! NO ...! NO ...!

NO ...! NO ...! NO ...! NO ...! NO ...!

NO ...! NO ...! NO ...! NO ...! NO ...!

NO ...! NO ...! NO ...! NO ...! NO ...!
NO ...! NO ...! NO ...! NO ...! NO ...!
NO ...! NO ...! NO ...! NO ...! NO ...!
NO ...! NO ...! NO ...! NO ...!'

... and stamped on them with his pointy, piggy little feet.

If they didn't get a move on, they weren't going to make it to the docks in time.

'Tell you what,' Jeff said. 'We're running a bit late, so maybe I could just flutter out and get you something new! Something to make you look very, you know, brave and ...'

'And dashing?' Handsome asked hopefully.

'Yeah! Brave and dashing.'

'And bold?'

'Definitely.'

'And heroic?'

'Yup. I'll get you something that makes you look brave, dashing, bold AND heroic. I know just the place.'

★

One hour and fifteen minutes later, Piggy Handsome and Jeff found themselves on top of another high roof – this time though, it was the roof of the depot at the docks.

'I CANNOT *BELIEVE* THIS IS WHAT I HAVE TO WEAR!' Handsome roared.

His outfit *was* rather unusual. Sure, the silver eye mask was probably quite fitting for someone about to embark on a daring rescue mission.

It was the tutu Piggy Handsome was so mad about.

As pink as candy floss, and as delicate as gossamer, the ruffles flittered in the breeze.

'Sorry, pal,' Jeff said. 'I went right through the toy box at number fifteen, and this was really the

only item of clothing I could find that would fit over your bu ...'

Handsome trembled with rage.

'... Er, bandage,' Jeff said quickly. 'But even if it's not the most daring, brave, bold, heroic look, you're still really ... *pretty*.'

Jeff stuck one leg in his feathers, while Piggy Handsome twitched and bristled like an electric toothbrush.

'I suppose at least I'm not entirely clothes-less,' he muttered under his breath after a while.

'Aaaaaaanyway ...' Jeff said. 'What's the plan?'

'Listen very carefully, Jeffry,' Handsome commanded. 'The plan is this: using a complicated selection of clips, harnesses and ropes, you will lower me through that skylight over there.'

Handsome pointed to the open skylight. Jeff hopped over to it, and peeped through.

'It's a very long way down, Handsome,' he said.

Piggy Handsome talked over him.

'Complete silence is absolutely *essential*,' he continued loudly. 'The villains must NOT be aware of my arrival.'

Handsome hadn't really thought this through,

of course. Silence was one thing, but it was summer, and so it was still bright daylight. If there was one thing likely to catch a human's eye, it was the glint of a ginger guinea pig, wearing a bright pink tutu, swinging from a rope and slowly descending from the ceiling.

'All right,' Jeff said. 'So did you pack a complicated selection of clips, harnesses and ropes?'

'No,' Handsome replied. 'Did you?'

'No,' said Jeff.

'Well, that's just *typical*.'

Jeff popped his head into the plastic bag

Handsome had brought with him. It had 'Rescue Mission Essentials' scrawled on the side in biro.

'So what *did* you bring, then?' Jeff asked.

Handsome snatched the bag. 'Er ...' he said, rooting around with his paw. 'I brought the nearly four pounds, and this talkie-walkie thingy, and these!'

He was holding his human's mobile phone, and a packet of Custard Creams.

'Right,' Jeff sighed, 'we're going to need a new plan. And it starts with using the door to get inside the depot.'

★

Inside the depot, the air was cool and smelled of metal. Piggy Handsome and Jeff trotted past gigantic containers, crates and machinery.

'Okay,' Jeff said, splitting open the packet of Custard Creams. 'We'll stay out of sight. When the Dixons arrive, and once they're in position, we'll use a diversion tactic.'

'A what?' Handsome asked.

'We'll use these biscuits to lure the humans away from Bunty Mastiff,' Jeff explained. 'We'll throw them so they land precisely, er ... here.'

He scratched an 'X' on the concrete floor with his beak.

'Aha!' Handsome exclaimed. 'You can leave that part to me, Jeffry. It just so happens I'm an *excellent* shot. I must have inherited the genes of my Great-Great-Great-Great-Great Grandpapa,

Target Handsome. There was nothing he couldn't hit with a bow and arrow, you know. In fact, he once fired an arrow at an atom from a thousand paces, and sliced it right down the middle!'

'An atom?' Jeff said incredulously. 'That can't be right, can it?'

It wasn't right. Target Handsome had definitely *not* split an atom. He'd actually grazed the skin of a large tomato, from fourteen paces.

'Of course it's right!' Piggy Handsome insisted. 'So, yes. I'll have absolutely no problem throwing the biscuits to *exactly* the right spot.'

'Righto,' Jeff chirped. 'The point is, they need to land close enough for the humans to see them, but far enough away to make the humans step away from the dog to pick them up.

'And that's when we strike! When they bend over to get the biscuits, I'll swoop down from my hiding place and grab Bunty Mastiff's lead. Then you jump down too. I'll throw you the lead, and then you RUN, taking Bunty Mastiff to safety! I'll be fluttering right behind you.'

'Hmm,' Handsome looked thoughtful for a moment. 'How sure are you that this plan will work, Jeffry?'

'Not very,' Jeff replied honestly. 'It's a pretty terrible plan when you think about it. But I do have a back-up plan.'

'Which is?'

'It's another plan, in case the first plan doesn't work.'

'But what is the other plan?' Handsome was looking irritated.

'It's Plan B,' Jeff said. 'Plan A is the first plan, and Plan B is the other plan, which we can use if Plan A doesn't work.'

'And what IS plan B?' Handsome snapped.

'Duh!' Jeff laughed. 'I just said! It's the back-up plan!'

'Just tell me ...' Piggy Handsome shrieked, 'WHAT IS THE BACK-UP PLAN?'

'Oh! Gotcha. Plan B is ... we attack!'

'WHAT?'

'Yeah,' Jeff said. 'I'll peck one of 'em on the nose, and you hit the other one with this dusty twig.'

Jeff pulled a tiny dusty twig out from beneath his wing.

'What? But . . . I . . .'

Suddenly, from the other end of the depot, came 'orrible voices.

And 'orrible footsteps.

'EEP!'

'They're coming!' Jeff tweeted. 'Quick, get into position.'

Custardomisation!
or The myriad things you can do with biscuits

'Soon we'll have everything we've ever wanted!'

Dolly's screechy, high-pitched voice echoed through the depot like ... like an out-of-tune violin being played by a cactus.

'YEAH! Even *more* than we've ever wanted!'

Dan replied. 'Like banjos and garden forks and cakes made out of hedgehogs! I bet there's stuff we don't even *know* we want yet! But when we realise we want it, we can just go out and get it, with our six hundred grand!'

'*Five* hundred grand,' Dolly corrected him.

'Eh?' Dan said, scratching his chin. 'I thought we said we wanted *six* hundred grand, or the dog gets it.'

Next to him, Bunty Mastiff (one banana horn hanging ever so sadly) gave a long, loud sigh.

'Nope,' said Dolly innocently, being sure not

to look her twin brother in the eye. 'Definitely ONLY five hundred grand, and we'll split it half and half. Fifty-fifty. Even stevens. You'll get a whopping two hundred grand, Dan! And so will I.'

'Oh, er . . .' Dan paused. 'Brilliant!'

Dolly sniggered to herself. 'Hurry up, you huge, hairy mutt,' she snapped at Bunty.

High above Dan and Dolly Dixon, on top of

a red, metal container the size of a lorry, Piggy Handsome and Jeff stayed well out of sight.

They waited and watched.

'Good grief, Jeffry!' Handsome whispered. 'Why have they brought a cow with them?'

'That's Bunty Mastiff!' Jeff hissed back. 'In disguise.'

'Ohhhh. Bunty Massive really is absolutely MASSIVE, isn't she?'

'Right, they're just where we want them,' Jeff said quietly. 'Are you ready to do your stuff with the biscuits?'

'Yes, indeedy!' Piggy Handsome grabbed a Custard Cream, being careful not to make the packet rustle.

'Now, the key to hitting a target is something that I like to call "aim", Jeffry,' Handsome explained confidently. Jeff rolled his eyes.

'It's all about mathematics really,' Handsome continued. 'While I'm speaking to you, I'm also, in my head, doing a range of very complex sums, to calculate the precise trajectory this biscuit will take. For example, I'm considering the angle at launch, the speed it will travel through the air, and the gravitational pull of planet Earth itself.'

Below, Dan Dixon was picking his nose and Dolly Dixon was tapping her scuffed, scruffy old shoe on the ground impatiently. Neither had noticed the 'X' scratched on the floor nearby.

Handsome was still jabbering.

'All of these things will ultimately affect where the biscuit lands, you see. Which will be precisely on that "X". Yes! I've done all the calculations, I'm ready! This really is an absolutely *amazing* skill, Jeffry. Watch and learn.'

Jeff did watch.

But he didn't learn.

Piggy Handsome lifted the biscuit up, high behind his head, and squinted in concentration before . . .

FWAPPPPPP!!

The Custard Cream hit Dolly Dixon right in the face.

'OW! Eh?'

'Oh . . . er . . . I . . .' Piggy Handsome mumbled, quickly taking another biscuit from the packet.

FWAPPPPPP!

The next Custard Cream smacked Dan Dixon

in the eye.

'OUCH! Wha—?'

FWAPPPPPP!

'Handsome, what are you DOING?' Jeff shouted.

FWAPPPPPP!

FWAPPPPPP!

FWAPPPPPP! FWAPPPPPP! FWAPPPPPP! FWAPPPPPP! FWAPPPPPP!

Piggy Handsome, mightily frustrated that his calculations had let him down, began lobbing those Custard Creams at a terrific speed.

One by one, they rained down on the Dixons – explosion after explosion of crumbs and vanilla goo.

As you'd expect of two people suddenly being pelted in the face with Custard Creams, Dan and Dolly Dixon both turned, and looked up, to see where on earth the missiles were coming from.

It took a moment for their brains to believe what their eyes were seeing: an absolutely *livid* ginger guinea pig in a bright pink tutu.

'What the ...?' Dolly screamed. 'It's that stinking rodent!'

'Let's get him!' Dan roared.

'EEEEP!'

'Wa!' yelped Piggy when he realised he'd been seen. He raced along the length of the container and attempted to skid to a halt, but actually skidded right off the end.

'Uh-oh!' Jeff watched in horror as Dolly swiped the air with her jagged, brown fingernails. She grazed Piggy Handsome's little toe, but couldn't quite get a grasp.

Handsome plopped to the ground, his tutu cushioning his fall.

'Come 'ere, you lousy little . . .'

'Run, Handsome, RUN!' Jeff yelled.

Huffing and puffing, Piggy Handsome hauled himself up and began to dart off in zig-zags, narrowly avoiding being flattened by Dolly's stomping feet.

'You go that way!' Dan yelled to his sister.

'And I'll block his path!'

'Help, Jeffry!' Handsome wailed.

Jeff glanced at the dusty twig, lying uselessly on the floor.

'Oo-er . . .' Jeff said to himself. 'I think it might be time for Plan C!'

He quickly fluttered inside Handsome's Rescue Mission Essentials bag and flipped over the mobile phone.

There was only one thing for it.

Yup, you guessed it.

He was jolly well going to call the police.

Conundumb!
or Mystery solved
(with the help of a tiny blue budgie)

The mood at Gibblesby Police Station was as grey as a midday shadow.

'RIGHT!' a stiff, upright human called Sergeant Noclue bellowed. 'Let's go over the facts AGAIN, shall we?'

Next to her, Constable Shift shuffled some papers, and cleared his throat.

'Well,' he began, 'we're pretty sure that Bunty Mastiff has been taken by the escaped twin convicts, Dan and Dolly Dixon.'

'And what makes you so sure?' Shift's superior snapped.

'When we rang the phone number on the ransom note, the man who answered said: "Hello, Dan Dixon speaking!" which led us to believe that we were speaking to Dan Dixon.'

'Mmhmmmmmmmmmmmmmmmmmm ...'

Sergeant Noclue nodded thoughtfully.

Constable Shift continued: 'We told Dan they had to give themselves up or else, and he replied . . .'

There was a pause while Shift checked his notes.

'Ah, yes. He said: "We'll NEVER give ourselves up, 'cos we're Dan and Dolly Dixon, so get us our six hundred grand and then go and SHOVE A CHRISTMAS TREE UP YER NOSE!"'

'SO!' Sergeant Noclue shouted (as she had a habit of doing). 'We know that Bunty Mastiff is with Dan and Dolly Dixon, but why haven't we FOUND them?'

'Well, this is where we're stumped!' Constable Shift sighed. 'We've circulated photographs and detailed descriptions of Dan and Dolly, *and* the dog – but no one's seen a thing!'

'If only it was a cow we were searching for!' came a voice from across the room. Constable Fuzz popped her head round her computer screen, chuckling.

'Have you seen this? There's this cow called Bog Off in the news. Her owners like taking her for walks on a lead. See! Just look at the photos on the *Gibblesby Herald* website – she's been spotted all over the place!'

'Oh yes!' chortled Sergeant Noclue. 'I saw her in the paper just this morning! How funny, a cow on a lead!'

Honestly. It was really a wonder how *any* crimes got solved in Gibblesby-on-Sea. *Ever.*

The Sergeant and Constable Shift went and looked at the computer screen. Constable Fuzz clicked through all the photos.

'Look! There's Bog Off in the supermarket! And there she is at the beach! And there she is climbing over a wall into someone's back garden! And there she is . . .'

BRRRRNNNGGG!

Constable Fuzz was interrupted by the sound of the telephone.

'Good afternoon!' she said, swiping up the receiver. 'Gibblesby Police Station, how may we help you?'

There was a pause while Constable Fuzz listened. 'This is odd,' she said, pressing a button to put the call on loud speaker. 'Listen.'

Sergeant Noclue and Constable Shift leaned in to hear a stream of curious squeaks and bangs coming from the telephone ...

TWEET!   Clank.   Eeeeeeeeeeeep!   TWEET

TWEET! Doinnnng! Clank.

Then far-away echoey voices:

'Where's he gone?'

'These docks ain't that big, we'll find him!'

'Get the massive dog to sniff him out!'

'That rodent's gonna get it, or my name ain't Dan Dixon! There he is, Dolly! Grab him!'

Then the line went dead.

'It's them!' gasped Constable Shift. 'That was Dan and Dolly Dixon!'

'And I deduce they've probably got Bunty Mastiff with them!' Constable Fuzz added.

'And they said they were at the docks,' Sergeant Noclue yelled. 'I think we should go and make some arrests!'

Hullabuffoonery!
or The daredevil chapter with the runaway fork-lift truck

'Now you're for it, you ratty-faced weasel!'

Having been chased outside, Piggy Handsome found himself cornered.

He was on top of a pile of crates. Beyond the crates, enormous container ships floated monstrously on the sparkling water. And below him, Dan and Dolly Dixon were giving him the proper evils. Neither of them were holding Bunty Mastiff's lead any more, but she was still standing silently next to them.

Jeff fluttered out and landed next to his friend.

'Oh, Handsome! Are you all right, pal?' he asked.

'No,' Piggy Handsome puffed. 'I'm most certainly NOT all right. This human is *extremely* rude! She keeps trying to grab me by my fluffy bits! LOOK WHAT SHE'S DONE TO MY QUIFF!

And she said she's going to feed me to tigers, or turn me into a toupee, whatever the lollipop that is!'

A toupee is a type of wig, in case you didn't know – and boy, oh boy, Dolly Dixon really looked like she meant it.

'He's got nowhere to go now!' Dan Dixon laughed.

'EEEP!'

Dolly lunged towards Piggy Handsome, who pressed himself against the wall, just a whisker's breadth out of reach.

'Hurry up, sis! It's already half past five, and we need to find the muppets who're bringing us all that lovely cash for the dog!'

Ah, of course! Dan and Dolly still had no idea it was Piggy Handsome and Jeff who'd sent the message (OR that they'd actually brought less than four quid with them).

'We'll find them in a minute,' Dolly replied, as she stretched, stretched, streeeeeeetched ... 'I'll just ...'

'There's nothing else for it, Jeffry!' Piggy Handsome gasped. 'I'm going to have to ...'

'No, Handsome!' Jeff shouted. 'Don't say it! Don't do it!'

'KUNG-FU!'

Oh dear.

'HYYYYWWWAAAAAA!'

Handsome's hips began twitching this way and that. His head jerked and bopped.

Roly poly.

Star jump.

Half-cartwheel.

Bendy-knee-bendy-knee.

Chop-chakka-chakka-chop paws.

'STAY STILL!' Dolly demanded.

'Is he having some sort of ... funny turn?' Dan asked.

'Or dancing the Cha-Cha?' asked Dolly.

'GOTCHA!'

It was one star jump too many. Dolly swiped!
And grabbed Piggy Handsome's little toe with a
pincer-like grip.

'EEEEEEPPPPP!'

'TWEET! Get off him!'

Jeff pecked Dolly hard on her knobbly knuckle
but she didn't even flinch. That crazy, cackling
crow face began dragging Handsome towards her.

'No! NO!' Jeff flapped in panic. He was about
to go in for the nose tweak, when he noticed Bunty

Mastiff was ... well, it looked very much like she was winking at him. She was nodding towards something too.

Jeff followed Bunty's gaze, and he knew exactly what that clever dog-cow was trying to tell him the instant he saw it.

A fork-lift truck.

With the key still in it.

Jeff had to do something fast. Dolly Dixon was dangling Handsome by his toe, eyeballing him like some sort of evil eagle.

'Let go of me, you *fiend*! You can't just hang

creatures upside down, you know, it can cause *migraines*. HAVE YOU NO MANNERS?'

It all took less than a second: Jeff pecked Piggy Handsome's knee.

'OWEEEEE!'

The shock of the peck made Handsome kick hard, as if he'd been jolted by a lightning bolt.

The foot that wasn't in Dolly Dixon's hand shot, momentarily, *right* up her nose.

'AARGHFFFPT!'

The shock of having a guinea pig's foot rammed up her nose was enough to make

Dolly Dixon let go of Piggy Handsome.

As Handsome began to fall, Jeff flew at his friend with all his might, collided with him mid-air

DUFFFTT!

and knocked him straight into the fork-lift truck,

where he bounced off a pedal and on to the seat.

'Quick!' Jeff yelled. 'Turn that knob thingy!'

Handsome did as instructed, while Jeff tweaked a lever. The machine rumbled into life and jerked forwards, its forks at the front rising as it went.

'What the . . . ?'

'AARGH!'

Dan and Dolly Dixon turned to get out of the way of the fork-lift, but it was already going at full pelt. A moment later, it scooped the Dixons up by their grimy collars, lifting them high into the air as it picked up speed.

'WAAAAAAHHHHHHHHHHHHH!'

With arms a-flailin' and legs a-swingin', they were a right couple of jiggly wrigglers.

'I don't know how to stop it, Jeffry!' Handsome shrieked as the fork-lift truck hurtled towards a pyramid of very heavy looking crates.

'You steer!' Jeff yelled. 'I'll try all those knobs and switches!'

Piggy Handsome leapt on to the steering wheel and, using his own weight, managed to heave the thing to the right. The truck careered around a corner on two wheels, then slammed down again, before racing on.

'HELP! HELP!' Dan Dixon squealed.

What a hullabaloo.

MNNNNNEEEEEEEEEEEENNNNG! the engine screamed.

HONK! A nearby boat sounded.

VARRM! VARRM! The forks jerked up and down as Jeff pecked and tweaked various buttons and levers.

The truck wasn't slowing down. It was speeding up and heading towards the edge of the dock, with Bunty Mastiff – strangely enough – running silently alongside.

'Do something, Jeffry!' Handsome squeaked. *'Do something!'*

'Er, I . . . !'

Suddenly, as light as a sugar puff, Bunty Mastiff leapt through the air and landed neatly on the fork-lift truck's seat. She plunged one enormous paw on to a pedal on the floor. The truck stopped

instantly, flinging Dan and Dolly Dixon up, up, up, over the edge of the dock and . . .

'OOFFFT!'

'DURGHHH!!'

They landed in a heap on top of a brown wooden crate.

'Phew!' Jeff fluffed his feathers. 'That was a bit close!'

Piggy Handsome peeled himself off the plastic windscreen.

'You . . . flippin' . . . FEATHER FACE!' Piggy Handsome screamed, brushing himself down and adjusting his quiff. 'You nearly got us killed!'

'Actually,' said Jeff, 'I helped you to save Bunty Mastiff.'

'Oh,' Handsome said, holding out a paw. 'Hello, Miss Massive.'

Bunty simply nodded at him.

'Ha! Now you're for it!' Dolly Dixon screeched as she stood up shakily. 'Come on, Dan, let's get that rodent once and for all!'

Dan heaved himself upright.

'Nah, forget him, Dolly,' he groaned. 'Grab the dog! We've got a ransom to collect!'

'I'm not letting that flea-ball get away with this!'

'But the dog's worth six hundred grand! What if she runs off?'

'If she does run off, it'll be YOUR fault. Why did you let go of the lead, anyway, you plank?'

''Cos you told me we had to get the stinking rodent ...'

'Hang on ... we're moving! Wait! Wait! Wait! Nooooooooo!'

'Oh. Well that's just *brilliant.*'

Handsome, Jeff and Bunty watched the bickering Dixons as they floated further ... and

further . . . and further . . . away.

You see, the crate they'd landed on was on a boat. It had the words 'Svalbard–Gibblesby–Svalbard' painted on the side – and it had just set sail.

'It's lucky for them they landed on a boat full of Gibblesby's finest wool jumpers,' Jeff chuckled, reading the sign on the crate, "cos it looks like those two horrible humans are off to the Arctic!'

MerryGoHound!
or The big 'saved' dog *finally speaks*

'I did it, Jeffry!' Piggy Handsome was clapping his paws together, running in circles round his friend. 'I saved Bunty Massive! The most valuable dog in the world!'

Jeff pecked hungrily at one of Bunty Mastiff's

discarded banana horns.

'Soon I shall have her safely back with her owners,' Handsome continued. 'And they'll say: "Ooh, *look!* This amazingly brave and handsome guinea pig just saved our absolutely MASSIVE dog! And they'll ring up Gibblesby TV News, and take pictures on their phones and send them to the internetters and . . .

'Oh, Miss Massive! I haven't even introduced myself properly, have I?' Handsome gave a polite bow. 'Piggy Handsome, your *hero*! Incredibly dashing guinea pig at your service. You must be delighted, I'm sure!'

Bunny Mastiff stayed silent.

'Right, well,' Handsome babbled. 'The plan from here is very simple. I shall hold your lead, and we will walk back into town, and jolly well get you home. You are SAVED!'

'Miss Massive? Aren't you going to say anything?'

'She might be more inclined to say something,' Jeff whispered, 'if you stop getting her name wrong. It's Bunty MASTIFF, not Massive.'

'Ashngny, gat's got gy ngane,' said Bunty.

'Pardon?'

Bunty lowered her head to the ground, and opened her mouth. Out from it dropped a silver-grey rock, which landed with a

C-CLACK

on the dock.

'I said, actually, that's not my name.'

Bunty's deep, soft voice sounded gentle and wise.

'Good grief, Jeffry!' Piggy handsome blurted. 'I haven't gone and saved the wrong diddling dog, have I?'

'No, no,' said Bunty. 'I mean, it's not my *real* name. Bunty Mastiff is the name given to me by the humans who bought me. But my real name – my spiritual name – is Dorg-Khyi. In Tibet, it means "nomad dog".'

'Oh yeah!' Jeff said. 'You're a Tibetan Mastiff. That's good, ain't it? Having a spiritual name!'

'And, erm,' said Piggy Handsome, pointing at the rock, 'what's *this* for?'

'That's Squeaky. My pet rock.'

'Pet rock?'

'She comes with me everywhere,' Bunty sighed. 'She makes me feel connected to my homeland – the wild Tibetan mountains.

'For years, my human bought me rubber toys and I *hated* them. Each time I picked up one of those toys, it would honk like an undignified donkey. "Go and get Squeaky!" my human would say. "Bring me Squeaky!" And each time, I brought her this rock. But she never understood.'

'Nice to meet you, Squeaky!' Jeff chirped at the rock.

For the first time in a very long time, Bunty Mastiff did the dog version of grinning (meaning, as you probably know, she wagged her tail).

'Well, that's very good but, anyway, let's go!' Handsome commanded. 'If I get you home soon, I might even make a little slot on this evening's news!'

Bunty's face dropped.

'Thank you, Mr Handsome,' she said solemnly. 'I am honoured that you tried to help me. But I do not want to be saved and returned to my owners. They keep me indoors and they tug at my fur with grooming brushes, then drag me along to horrible dog shows . . .'

'You WHAT?' Piggy Handsome yelled. 'You *have* to let me take you back! I saved you from the Dixons!'

'The truth is,' Bunty said, 'I went along with those two dreadful humans deliberately. That house, it was a prison! In stealing me, they *freed* me. I allowed them to dress me as a cow – I even mooed a bit yesterday. You see, if I'd been spotted,

I would have been "saved" and returned.

'All this time, though, I've been hoping to escape to my true home, where my howl will echo around the mountains, where I can roam free with the herds. I've been waiting for my chance because, well . . . my *instinct* is calling me to Tibet.'

'Yes! And THIS is your chance!' Jeff shouted. 'You see, Handsome! I *told* you! You can't argue with instinct!'

'NOPE!' Handsome blustered, marching back and forth. 'I'm not having this! I have spent an *entire* afternoon saving you, Bunty Massive. Two hours from now, I will be a news headline: "HERO GUINEA PIG!" I saved you, fair and square.'

'Tibet – that's somewhere near China, isn't it?' Jeff was all aflutter.

'It is,' Bunty replied.

'Well, when we were larking about on the fork-lift . . .'

'HA!' Handsome snorted.

'I saw a ginormous ship that's heading to China. I know that 'cos it said Gibblesby–China–Gibblesby on the side. It's just down there – and it's loaded up, ready to go!'

Bunty gasped. 'I could find my way to Tibet from China! I'm *sure* I could.'

Suddenly, in the distance, sirens blared. There was a far-off flash of blue lights.

'Oh no, the police are coming!' gulped Jeff. 'I called them earlier and . . .'

'Excellent!' Piggy Handsome exclaimed. 'They will see me holding Bunty's lead, realise I've saved her, and give us a lift back to town, where all the reporters live.'

'Handsome,' Jeff said seriously. He nodded at Bunty, whose head was now hanging to her chest.

'But … but … I *saved* her!' Piggy Handsome spluttered.

'Maybe what you need to think about,' Jeff said quietly, 'is how you could *really* save her.'

All the fur on Handsome's neck bristled.

His fists curled into balls.

One eye twitched.

He was crosser than a …

'They'll make me go back,' Bunty whispered.

Piggy Handsome sighed.

'ARGH …! *Fine!*' he blurted. 'Let's find this ship.'

As the first police car rounded the corner into the docks, Piggy Handsome leapt on to Bunty's back, while she scooped up Squeaky in her mouth.

'This way!' Jeff took off, and flew straight along the edge of the dock.

Bunty ran like the wind, while poor Piggy Handsome clung on for all his tiny life was worth.

'PFFTTT!' Your fur! PFFFFT! It's in my face!' he squealed. 'EEEEP! You're going *terribly fast!*'

'There it is!' Jeff landed on top of a container, puffed and fluffed and bluer than ever against the greying sky. In front of them, an absolute whopper of a container ship was being de-anchored.

Bunty lay down gently, and Piggy Handsome slipped down her back to the ground.

'Ngangou,' Bunty said. 'Ngo, ngory,'

C-CLACK

The colossal white dog looked deeply into Piggy Handsome's eyes.

'Sorry. What I mean is, *thank you*,' she said.

'Yes, well ...' Handsome muttered. 'I'm *very* glad you appreciate it, because *actually* ...'

He didn't see it coming – Bunty's massive pink tongue,

CCCHLLLLLUP

with its very appreciative, heartfelt, and slobbery kiss.

'ARGHPPFT!! Get off me, you . . . !'

She'd already gone.

Leaving Squeaky behind, right next to Handsome's little toe, Bunty dashed to the edge of the dock, and disappeared out of sight.

'I'm going home!' Piggy Handsome stropped.

'So's she!' said Jeff. 'Let's just wait and see her off, eh?'

A few moments later, Jeff pointed with a wing.

'Look!' he said.

And there she was.

Bunny Mastiff, like a true mountain dog, was clambering up the containers and making her way to the top.

'We know you're here, and you're under arrest! So come out with your hands up!' At the other end of the dock, Sergeant Noclue and Constables Shift and Fuzz had no idea that Dan and Dolly Dixon were actually on a boat, already nearing the North Sea.

WOAAAARRRRRGGGNNN!

The container ship's horn sent fluff-and-
feather-frizzing vibrations through the air.

As the clouds broke, revealing a spectacular
golden sunset, the ship slowly moved out of the dock.

Right at the front, on top of the highest container, Dorg-Khyi stood as proud as a pineapple, her pure white, mane-like fur billowing in the sea breeze.

Piggy Handsome, quiet for once in his life, raised a sad little paw and waved.

'That was close!' Jeff chuckled. He nodded in the direction of the police, who were now calling out Bunty's name.

Piggy Handsome kept his eyes on the ship.

'Yes, I *was* close,' he sighed. 'I was so, SO close.'

ExAarrrgghhsperation!
or That 'right place, wrong time' fury

Back in the West Wing of their house, Piggy
Handsome was slouching in his opulent armchair.
He patted Squeaky, like the good pet rock she was,
and then scowled at Jeff Budgie.

'You should give yourself a pat on the back,' Jeff

said, munching his seeds. 'You did the right thing.'

'Yes, yes,' Handsome grumbled. 'I know I did the *right thing*. Bunty Massive or Dawgy whatever her name is, will find her way to Tibet, and she'll howl at great big mountains, and run about with actual cows, and finally discover what it is to be free.

'But what about meeeee? I was supposed to be a hero!'

'But you *are* a hero,' Jeff said kindly. 'You saved her from her prison!'

'What's the point of saving someone if no one KNOWS ANYTHING ABOUT IT?'

'Tomorrow's another day, Handsome,' Jeff replied cheerfully, tweaking on the telly. 'We'll come up with another way to get you famous, you mark my words. I mean, it can't be that hard, can it?'

'Not the television, Jeffry,' Handsome groaned.

'I don't want to watch the news tonight. I just can't bear to think of what might have been.'

Happy, twang-twang music floated out of the TV speakers.

'The news has already finished,' Jeff said. 'I was hoping there might be a replay of that darts match from earlier.'

'Welcome to another episode of *Pets With Sore Bits*,' a friendly voice said. 'And – well, this is very exciting! Tonight we are LIVE from . . .'

'The thing I don't understand,' Piggy Handsome said loudly over the telly, 'is why Bunty

Massive didn't just bark at her human, or even *sit* on her human, until it let her go.'

'She wasn't that type, though, was she?' Jeff replied, with one eye on the television. 'She seemed . . . peaceful. I suppose she was just waiting for a way to escape without hurting anyone's feelings, or frightening them. And it just so happened that Dan and Dolly Dixon going and pinching her like that gave her the chance to . . .'

Jeff suddenly gasped.

'I don't believe it!' he exclaimed.

'You don't believe *what?*' Handsome said sulkily.

'It's unbelievable!'

'*What's* unbelievable?'

'Ha! You'll *never* believe this, Handsome . . .'

Piggy Handsome stormed out of his maisonette, and stamped a pointy, piggy little foot.

'WHAT ... WON'T ... I ... BELIEVE?' he demanded.

'Banger's on telly! Look! And that must be Doctor Vethead!'

'Huh?'

Jeff pointed at the TV with his wing.

On the screen, Banger was in the reception of

the animal hospital, and a human in a white coat was just behind her.

Banger had very nearly, *almost* reached the exit. Just as the automatic door began to slide open, two pudgy human hands swooped down ... and scooped her up.

'And where do you think you're off to, you silly old thing?' Dr Vethead laughed, ruffling Banger's ears and turning her round to face the camera.

Banger sighed.

The presenter of the show – a human with frizzy brown hair and dangly kitten-shaped earrings – came into shot. 'And who's this cheeky pup?' she asked.

'This is Banger!' Doctor Vethead replied. 'A lovely little old sausage dog. She's been in hospital for two weeks now, having her heart monitored, so we ...'

'*I don't believe it*,' Piggy Handsome whispered in a trembly voice.

'I know! I told you it was a hospit—!'

'*Do you mean to tell me*,' Handsome fumed, 'that if we'd just stayed in that prison, I would be on live television, RIGHT NOW?'

'Erm . . .'

Jeff probably didn't think there was a right way to answer that question.

So he didn't answer it.

'Ohhhhh! Everything I've been through today!' Piggy Handsome howled. 'I could have just stayed in that wretched place, and waited for the CAMERAS TO TURN UP!'

Oh crumbs. Piggy Handsome marched over to the telly and slapped it.

'Why didn't you tell me?' Handsome screamed at on-screen Banger. '*Why didn't you tell me?*'

'She can't hear you, it's—' Jeff began.

'I've got a mind to . . . just you wait . . . you . . . utter . . . utter . . . BARNACLE!'

'Calm down, Handsome. Fancy having a game of—'

'Right. That's it! Follow me, Jeffry. We're

going back to the prison and we are BREAKING

BACK IN!'

Jeff Budgie shook his head and sighed.

He stretched his pretty blue wings.

Then stuck one leg in his feathers.

The End

So we leave Piggy Handsome still ranting and raving.

He did the right thing when the dog needed saving,

but the road to his dream — it seems so very far.

Well, he'll never give up! Not until he's a STAR!